Take A Chance

Miyeko May

To little me, who didn't think she could. You did it.

* * *

Author Note

"If they can learn to say Tchaikovsky, Dostoyevsky, &
Michelangelo, they can learn to say Uzoamaka"

- Uzo Aduba via Twitter

Hi I'm Miyeko. The first time I heard this quote it really resonated with me as I'm sure it did for a lot of people who have names that are not "the norm". But it was really important to me to have my name on my work because my work is a representation of me and so is my name. I will never be upset about accidental mispronunciations, all I ask is that you try. (:

So hello my name is Miyeko and it is pronounced (Me-yay-koh).

1

CASSANDRA

If the travel day I just had is any indication, I'm about to have a terrible vacation. Two delays, an almost missed connection, and a four hour flight filled with screaming and crying children is truly what travel nightmares are made of. Not to mention, someone's offspring decided my seat was a perfect place to kick their feet for most of my second flight. Needless to say, I was irritable and exhausted when I finally landed at my destination.

When I step off of the plane and feel the fresh warm air and bright sun against my brown skin, I can feel myself relax a little. I force myself to take some calming breaths to try to shake off my bad mood, because after all of the hassle of the day, I was on vacation in Mexico and I was not going to spend the next few days with a sour attitude. Growing up my family didn't have money for expensive vacations, they were a luxury so far out of our tax bracket that I didn't even take my first flight until college. Now that my finances allow me to travel, I always take an extra moment to appreciate it.

After entering the airport, I make my way through immigration and find my luggage without much issue. I text my sister Tiffany, to let her know that I landed safely. Tiffany is the entire reason that I am even on this vacation, and also the reason that I'm here alone. Tiffany is my sister but also my best friend, with less than two years in age separating us we grew up very close. As the temperatures decreased, we both decided that we needed a break from normal life and the impending brutal winter that was sure to come to the Midwest. So we booked a vacation to Mexico. Tiffany was going to leave her husband at home, and I was very much single so the plan was for us to enjoy a trip just the two of us. And then just two days before we were set to leave, Tiffany caught the flu.

The fever, chills, promising yourself you won't take your health for granted once it's over, version of the flu. But even while in bed, sick as hell, Tiffany was not having it when I told her that if she couldn't go, I wasn't going to go either. I argued that the trip was meant to be spent together, so it just wouldn't feel right without her, and we had very meticulously laid plans that I wanted to stick with. Tiffany didn't care about any of that, and countered all of my objections and reservations about going alone and insisted I go. She said that at the end of the day, I deserved the trip. And I couldn't argue with that. So now here I am standing outside an airport in Mexico, sweating out my edges.

"Welcome!" The doorman to the resort says as he opens the door to my taxi.

"Thank you," I reply with a smile.

The taxi driver pulls my suitcase out of the trunk and leaves it. The doorman takes my suitcase and rolls it behind him as we make our way to the entrance of the resort.

"Champagne?" Another resort worker asks me, a filled flute already in his extended hand.

Don't mind if I do.

I accept the flute with a smile and take a large gulp, the bubbly alcohol warming my body.

The check in process is smooth. A lovely woman at the front desk gets me squared away with my wristband and key cards, as well as a map of the resort and its restaurants. The worker who had been patiently waiting with my luggage leads me up to the elevator and calls it for me. When the doors open, he holds the door for me to step on with my suitcase.

"Please enjoy your trip, miss," he says with a smile before the doors close and the elevator begins to rise.

In my room the view from my balcony takes my breath away. The sun is starting to set over the ocean and it looks utterly unreal. I snap a few pictures on my phone that don't come any anywhere close to capturing the beauty of the sunset, before I flop onto one of the beds in my room with a contented sigh.

Doing things alone is unusual for me. In my day to day life, even though I enjoy my times of solitude, I spend a lot of time with my sister or my friends. With Tiffany and I so close in age, we usually do a lot of things together. We lived together until she got married a year ago, and even now we only live a few minutes away from each other. So traveling out of the country alone is a huge step for me and I promised Tiffany that I would try to take advantage of it.

My stomach loudly grumbles, reminding me that the only thing I've eaten recently was an overpriced airport fruit cup and the complimentary two pack of Biscoff cookies on the plane. I pull myself off the bed and into the bathroom to freshen up. I trade my comfy airport clothes for a short, flowy sundress and a pair of sandals to leave my room and go explore.

I have an early dinner by myself at one of the restaurants near my room. The food is absolutely delicious, including the best ceviche I have ever had. While I eat, I take in my scenery and do a bit of people watching. It seems like most of the people here are couples, most likely celebrating a big event of some sort, a honeymoon or anniversary possibly. There are also some families here too. A young couple with a toddler daughter sit close to me, and the little girl spends most of the meal waving hello to everyone around her.

When I finish my dinner, the sound of music draws me toward a patio and bar. There are string lights hung from the ceiling and upbeat music plays from hidden speakers, creating a great vibe. Exactly what I need after my long ass day. There are some people sitting at the various tables around the patio, and a few couples taking advantage of a small dance floor. At the bar itself, two bartenders work to make drinks, but only a single guy sits at the bar. His back is to me giving me an opportunity to check him out without being caught. I don't know how long it's been since I spent time with a man. I have long since given up on dating apps and meeting men out in the world who weren't assholes, creeps or both was not an easy feat. This mystery guy is wearing a cream shorts and polo set, the shirt fitting snugly on his biceps and the color complementing his deep brown skin well.

I step up to the bar and take a seat at one of the barstools a few seats away from the mystery guy. I force myself not to sneak looks in his direction and instead focus on getting one of the bartender's attention.

"Can I have a mojito please?"

The bartender nods and starts mixing up my drink.

I pull out my phone to take some quick pictures and video of the space to send to Tiffany later.

"Cassandra?" A smooth, deep voice asks from my right.

I shift my gaze over in the direction and find the man I had been ogling moments ago looking at me expectantly. I take in the features of his face that I hadn't been able to when I was creeping on him from behind. His lips catch my attention first, full and surrounded by a full beard that connects with a fresh line up.

This man was *fine*.

It's his eyes that keep my attention, golden pools of brown filled with humor in a way that almost seems familiar. Slowly his lips raise into a smirk and then recognition hits me.

Holy fuck.

I knew those damn kids were a bad omen.

2

CASSANDRA

After high school, I left my hometown without a second thought. I always knew that staying in Oak View was never the end goal for me, so when I found a way out in the form of a full ride scholarship to my top choice university, I took it. Tiffany was already going to school there, so really it was a no brainer for me. We traveled back to see our parents during our breaks, but after graduation neither of us moved back and instead we decided to stay in Rosewood together. One of the big benefits of moving away was being able to start fresh in a new place and leaving behind the people of the past. Yet, here the past was standing right in front of me in the form of Cyrus Levine.

Between middle school and high school, Cyrus and I practically grew up together, but I would never dare to consider us more than classmates. The Levine brothers were the epitome of "the popular kids" at our school. Blake and Cyrus were both tall, good looking, and athletic, effectively checking all the boxes to be sought after by the girls in our school. Blake was two grades ahead but Cyrus and I were in the same grade.

Cyrus was known to be a class clown of sorts, always wanting to get a laugh out of the people around him. Behind the funny jokes, Cyrus was also infuriatingly smart, the kind of academically gifted where new concepts and topics came easy to him. Which, unfortunately for me, left him a whole lot of time to get on my last nerve in whatever classes we had together. During our senior year we shared most of our classes, since by that time we had finished all of the required classes and were just left with the small pool of AP classes to choose from.

"Here you go," the bartender says, snapping me out of my thoughts.

I accept my mojito gratefully, taking a long swig before I turn my attention back to Cyrus, eyes narrowed.

"What are you doing here?" I ask accusatory.

"Damn you see a nigga for the first time in damn near a decade and thats the first thing you say?" he asks with a chuckle. "Same ole Mighty Mouse I see."

I press my lips together and roll my eyes at the nickname that he used to call me in high school. At some point over the years he adopted it, and no matter how many times I told him to drop it, he continued to use it. It's actually been closer to nine years since we've seen each other, not that I've been counting.

I turn away from Cyrus and take another sip from my drink, intent to ignore him. Just because we're in the same place doesn't mean that we have to interact right?

From the corner of my eye, I see Cyrus pick up his drink from the bar and carry it with him to close the purposeful gap I had put between us when I sat down. Cyrus doesn't seem to agree with my sentiment that we don't have to interact. He slides onto the barstool next to me, and when his knee brushes mine my body heats, electric energy flowing through me.

What the hell was that?

I know its been a minute since I've had any dick, but there is no possible way I'm feeling anything towards Cyrus fucking Levine. My lack of male interaction is clearly getting to me and my body is just reacting to anything. Yes, that has to be it.

"My brother is getting married this weekend."

"What?" I ask, shaking myself out of my thoughts again, but still confused on why he's giving me that information.

"You asked me why I was here. It's for my brother Blake's wedding."

"Oh wow congrats to him and his fiancée," I say sincerely.

"Yeah I got a nice ass vacation out of it so I can't complain," he replies, swirling his drink, some kind of dark liquor on the rocks, before he takes a sip.

"And what brings you here, Mighty Mouse?"

Again with that damn nickname.

"I'm just here for a vacation." I use the straw of my drink to move the ice and mint leaves around in the glass, avoiding looking at Cyrus.

"And where's your other half?" He asks, looking around us. "I'm sure if you're here then she isn't that far away."

I scoff, "What is that supposed to mean?!"

"It means that you and Tiff were damn near attached at the hip and I doubt that's changed now."

"Boy you don't know me," I huff.

"You're right I don't know you now," he says seriously, his eyes locked so intensely on mine that I'm forced to look away to break the tension I feel rising between us. "What do you say I get you another drink and then as old classmates we can catch up? So I can get to know THIS Cassandra."

My first instinct is to say no. I only planned to come here for one drink before I went back to my room for the night. I like plans, knowing what's next, and having things figured out. Plans work for me, they mean certainty and control which brings me comfort. But I can hear Tiffany's voice in my head telling me to live a little and let go of my plans. "We will never be this young and fine again so we might as well live it up," she always says.

So instead of giving the flimsy excuse I had already been

forming in my head, I say, "Okay".

3

CYRUS

Cassandra Scott. Of all the positives I knew this trip to Mexico would have, seeing Cassandra again for the first time in almost a decade was not one of them. She's gorgeous, but that doesn't surprise me in the slightest. In high school, Cassandra always had my attention, even though she was never checking for me. In school, she spent her time fully focused on academics. She was quiet and kept to herself and her small circle of friends.

I signal to the bartender to get his attention. "Can we get another round of these?"

"Of course," he replies, taking our empty glasses away with him.

With the drinks ordered, I take in this version of Cassandra that's in front of me. Long braids with loose strands of curly hair flow down her back to her ass. So much of her is the same, her large brown eyes and smooth brown skin. The beautiful smile that she flashed at the bartenders and the adorable scowl that she sends my way are both familiar. But for all the familiarity I see, there are also some things that are different between the girl I once knew years ago and the woman before me. A natural occurrence when you go from seeing someone nearly every day for years, to no contact at all.

And damn it if seeing her again after all these years doesn't stir up all the same feelings I had when we were teenagers.

"You're staring," she says plainly, cocking her head to the side.

I can't help but grin at her bluntness. "Forgive me." I say but keep my eyes locked with Cassandra's.

She gives a small eyeroll and looks away, but I catch the small smirk on her lips.

The bartender comes back with our fresh drinks and I give him a nod of thanks. Cassandra eagerly takes her drink, fiddling with the straw and pointedly not looking at me anymore.

"So Cass, what brings you to Mexico?"

"Just needed a break," she replies, tossing her braids over one shoulder. "Some time away from work and the realities of life. And the cold."

I chuckle, "Yeah the Midwest winters are brutal."

"Tell me about it. I could go the entire rest of my life without ever seeing snow again."

"I travel a lot for work and I would be lying if every time I'm in California, it didn't make me consider moving."

"What do you do for work?"

"I'm a pilot. I'm based in Indianapolis but I fly all over the country."

"So what's stopping you from moving then?"

I just look at her for a moment surprised by her blunt question before I reply.

"Besides a shit ton of paperwork to get a transfer with my company, nothing I guess. It just has never felt like the right move."

She nods in understanding.

"And what about you? What have you been up to since leaving Oak View?"

"I went to college with Tiffany and we ended up staying in

Rosewood. A few years after graduation, I started my small business there. It's a small skin care company."

I let out a low whistle. "Damn, that's amazing."

She cracks a smile, "Yeah Lovely Day is like my baby. It was rough for the first few years, but we're doing okay now."

"So why skin care?"

"I was tired of Black people, Black women especially being thought of last for everything. Sunscreen that leaves us looking like ghosts, foundation ranges that never have our shades. So I wanted to have a place where Black women are catered to."

"That's admirable as fuck. I mean don't get me wrong, I didn't doubt that you would do something great in life, but to do something great and that's specifically for people who look like us is amazing."

"Wow sis, your hair is sooo cute!" From behind us two women approach and excitedly start talking to Cassandra.

I sit back and sip my bourbon watching Cass. The other women are animated, talking loud and clearly more than a little intoxicated.

"We came over for shots but then I saw you and thought 'damn she's pretty'. Wait, you guys should definitely take a shot with us!" The woman rambles.

Cassandra looks over at me and I shrug, not opposed to joining.

"Fuck it, we'll take one."

One of the women excitedly claps her hands together. "Great! What should we take a shot of?"

"Tequila?"

I make a disgusted face at the suggestion.

"What? You too good for tequila?" Cassandra quips.

I laugh, "Nah I just usually stick to dark liquor."

"Fine. I'll take tequila and mister 'I only drink dark' can have whiskey."

Moments later the shots are placed in front of us with a

small dish of lime wedges.

The four of us hold our shot glasses up together and cheers.

I toss my shot back quickly, the liquor burning as it goes down. I catch Cass' face at the end of taking her own shot, her nose scrunched up as she sets down the shot glass to bite into her lime wedge.

A new song begins to play through the speakers around the bar. I'm unfamiliar with the song but I seem to be in the minority because a lot of other people cheer as the song begins. Cassandra starts to dance in her seat to the beat and even sings along.

I raise my eyebrows at her. "Oh this is your shit huh?"

"Hell yeah." She says, still dancing along in her seat.

"Okay, okay. What else is in your music rotation?"

She takes a second to think about my question. "I think it depends on the day and what mood I'm in. I can listen to anything from Rod Wave to Carrie Underwood slashing tires. Probably the most consistent is 2000s R&B though."

"I mean for good reason, the music from the 2000s and 2010s is top tier."

"Right! Tiffany and I would listen to Bow Wow on repeat. And I guarantee if you play No Hands or We Belong Together at any function, it'll be lit."

I chuckle, "Aight, since you're into music, I got a question for you."

She takes a sip from her drink before she sits back and looks at me again. "Go for it."

"Who has the hardest verse on No Hands?"

Without even thinking about it she responds, "Roscoe, no question?"

"Roscoe!?"

I widen my eyes in surprise. "You're really choosing Roscoe? The nigga who just spells his name and has that wack ass bologna line?"

"Okay, so who you voting for then? Waka Flocka?"

"Absolutely not. Wale has the best lyrics out of the three of them and its not even a question."

Cass scoffs. "Okay but nobody's listening to No Hands for the lyrics, they're listening to get lit. And for me personally, Roscoe's part will always make me want to shake my ass."

I let out a loud laugh at Cassandra's bluntness. It takes me by surprise, because at least back in the day, she was way more reserved.

"You know what, I can't even argue with that." I concede.

The conversation continues easily between us. I can see Cassandra relax more as the night carries on, possibly from the liquor.

"And it was your fault!," she says laughing. "I had never gotten a detention before, but you just had to drag me into your mess."

"Nah Mrs. Washington was always on that with me." I defend. "I was just innocently trying to ask for help on the assignment."

"From across the classroom!"

"Well yeah, why would I bother asking anyone else when I could ask the smartest person in the class, which just so happened to be you. And you *just* so happened to be across the room."

"Yeah yeah whatever."

In reality, I hadn't really needed help on that assignment in Mrs. Washington's class, but back then I took any chance I could get to talk to Cassandra. And I had no regrets, even with the detention.

Cass lets out a deep yawn. When I look down at my watch, I realize that its been damn near three hours since I sat down at the bar.

"It's late, I should probably head back to my room."

"Okay, I'll walk with you."

Cass rolls her eyes and laughs, "I'm perfectly capable of getting to my room, Cyrus."

"I know, I just want to make sure you're good. Can I do that?"

With a sigh she relents and I let her lead the way to her room.

We walk in silence but close enough that I can smell her perfume. It's sweet and floral and I love it. Every few steps our fingers brush and I stop myself from taking her hand. My entire body is vibrating, probably at least partially from the liquor, but I also know that a large part of it is because of the girl beside me.

Cass stops in front of one of the doors and turns to me. "This one is me."

"Thank you for having that drink with me."

She nods. "Have a good night."

I smile to myself at her words. Whether she knows it or not, I already had a great night, because of her.

4

CYRUS

"Who are you looking for?" My future sister in law, Maia, asks me as she steps up behind me in the line for the breakfast buffet.

I bring my attention away from sweeping around the terrace to look at Maia. "What are you talking about?"

We slowly move through the line, serving ourselves from various pans heaped with food, my stomach rumbling.

"You've been scanning the room since we got here. It's obvious you're looking for someone."

"Whatever you say," I reply noncommittally.

But in reality Maia is right. After last night, I can't stop thinking about Cassandra. The odds of both of us being here, at the exact resort at the exact same time, are so dismally low that I've been questioning whether or not I made up last night entirely. But then I remember the electricity that I felt when I was with her, and I know for damn sure that it was real. That, and the damn pounding happening in my head from being up far too late and drinking far too little water.

My brother Blake and his fiancee Maia have been dating for years, so it was no surprise when he proposed. It was a surprise when they decided that, instead of getting married in the states, they wanted to have a destination wedding in Mexico. The bridal party only consists of me as Blake's best man and Maia's two sisters as her maids of honor. At the request of the bride and groom, the bridal party and some of their closest friends flew out early to have some pre-wedding fun and activities.

I'm one of the first people in our group to get back to the table with my plate. I sit down and start eating, but still can't help looking around the room.

"Who you looking for bro?"

Damn is it that fucking obvious?

Blake pulls out a chair at the table for Maia to sit before he takes the chair next to me for himself.

"So I'm not trippin, you see it too right!" Maia exclaims. "I tried to ask him in line but he got all defensive."

I shake my head and try to ignore both of them, instead focusing on eating my breakfast.

"I don't know what y'all are talking about. I'm just trying to eat my food."

Maia lets out an unconvinced noise, but they both don't push anymore as more people from our group join us at the table. Altogether there are seven of us: Blake and Maia, Alana and Amber, Maia's sisters, Damian and Will, two of Blake's close friends, and me.

"Have you seen mom and dad yet?"

I shake my head no at Blake's question. "Nah but you know mom was probably up at the crack of dawn to fuss at the worker's about making sure everything is perfect for tonight."

"Yeah I saw them yesterday when they first got here and I told her not to worry so much, but she wasn't tryna hear that."

Maia carefully crafted an itinerary for the trip that included both group excursions and down time when we could all enjoy the relaxation of the resort and beach. Today we have the morning and afternoon to ourselves before a welcome dinner for everyone coming to the wedding tomorrow.

As we finish eating, the question of what everyone plans to do with their free time circles around the table.

"I just want to lay out by the pool honestly," Alana replies when someone asks what she planned to do.

"Oooo, can you save me a spot too?" Maia asks. "I need to go grab my sunglasses from our room, I forgot them."

"Of course, as long as another old lady doesn't try something."

We all laugh, remembering the scene from the previous day when an older woman tried to take Maia's chair when she went to the bathroom, and was two seconds away from getting cursed out.

"Aye Cy, you tryna check out the pool volleyball game? It starts in like ten minutes." Will asks.

"Yeah I'm down."

Blake and Maia leave together to head back to their room. The rest of us leave the table and head out towards the pool, stopping first to grab towels from the towel stand. The pool is large and surrounded by palm trees and lounge chairs. Towards one end, there's a bar with both swim up and walk up options, and near the middle of the pool, a worker is tying up the net for the daily afternoon pool volleyball.

"Come with me to get a drink," Amber says, tugging Alana's arm towards the poolside bar.

The girls go off in the direction of the bar while me, Will, and Damian head toward the pool itself. Like yesterday, most of the loungers are occupied, or at least have a towel or someone's belongings on them. I look around taking it all in. And then I see her.

Cass is laid out on a lounge chair near the bar in a bright yellow bikini that looks amazing against her brown skin. One of the pool bartenders stops by her chair and kneels down to hand her a drink from his serving tray. When she notices him, her face lights up in a smile.

"Yo, I'll get up with y'all in a minute," I call out to Damian and Will. I quickly walk away before either of them can ask me any questions.

5

CASSANDRA

From my balcony, I have the perfect view of the beach and the clear blue water, it's truly breathtaking. This morning, I decided to sleep in and had room service deliver me breakfast on my balcony instead of going down to the buffet. I sip my mimosa and eat my breakfast before I get myself ready.

After showering and moisturizing, I open my suitcase and look through the swimsuits I brought with me. In the full length mirror, I alternate between an olive green one piece with cutouts and a mustard yellow two piece, holding them both up to my body. I decide on the yellow, loving how the color pops against my skin. The fit is perfect, showing just the right amount of skin. I don a pair of sunglasses, slide on my sandals, and make my way down to the pool.

Initially when Tiffany and I booked the trip, we planned to do some excursions together, but now that it was just me, I decided that staying at the resort and simply enjoying a few days of relaxation was more than okay with me. I weave through the lounge chairs until I find one that is unoccupied and spread my towel out on it.

Before long, one of the pool waiters stops by my chair to ask if he can get me anything. The waiter comes back quickly with the fruity cocktail I ordered and I take it from him with a smile.

I take a few sips of my drink and lay back in my chair, closing my eyes to the sun.

Suddenly, I'm covered in shade, the cool breeze of the ocean giving me goosebumps from the lack of direct sunlight.

I open my eyes and lift my sunglasses to see what happened, and I lock eyes with Cyrus. He's wearing navy swim trunks and a crisp white tee, a gold rope chain peeking out from the neckline.

"Good morning," he says with a smile.

"Good morning Cyrus." I reply trying to keep my features neutral, but I can tell I've failed when his smile grows.

He takes a seat at the end of my chair.

"Sure just make yourself comfortable," I say with a sarcastic laugh.

He shoots me another grin. "Thank you for the invitation."

I roll my eyes at him and shake my head.

From behind Cyrus, I see a man and woman walking this way holding hands. As they approach I recognize Blake, Cyrus's brother, which must mean the woman with him is his fiancée.

Blake places his hand on Cyrus's shoulder, "Man bro, I thought you and the guys were playing the game."

"I was but then I ran into Cass, you remember her right?"

Blake nods at me.

"Hell yeah, good to see you Cass."

Blake's fiancée looks between me and Cyrus with her eyebrows raised before saying, "so this is who you were breaking your neck to look for at breakfast."

Cyrus chuckles and shakes his head. "And little miss big mouth over there is my sister in law Maia."

I give Maia a small wave and she returns it with a wave and a smile.

"Just one more day until it's official."

"Congratulations!"

"Yeah, yeah, now everyone knows everyone, weren't you guys going to the bar or something," Cyrus says clearly trying to get them to leave.

"Aye y'all playing or what? The game is about to start and we need more players" Another guy who I assume is one of their friends, asks coming up behind Maia and Blake.

"I'm down, but I think Cy is a little occupied," Blake jokes. Cyrus shoots him an annoyed look, and I can't help but laugh.

"If you guys need another player, I'm down to join in," I offer.

"Nah you don't have to Cass, I'm sure they can find someone else."

"You aren't scared of a little competition are you Cyrus?" I ask with a raised eyebrow, standing from my seat.

I catch his gaze on my thighs before he slowly raises his eyes to reach mine.

"Ooooo," Blake and their friend call out.

"I like her already, I'm calling dibs on her for my team" Maia says, linking her arm in mine and leading us over to where the pool volleyball game is set up.

As we walk away, I look back over my shoulder and see Cyrus watching me. His usual humorous gaze is gone and instead there's heat in his eyes. My nipples betray me and harden at the intensity of his stare.

In the water, we split off into teams, and I end up on a team with Maia and Blake. Cyrus is on the other team with their friends, Will and Damian, and both of our teams are rounded out with other people on vacation at the resort. The resort worker in charge of refereeing the game tosses the ball over to the other team and the games begin.

"Mine!" I call out to my teammates as I set the ball towards a blonde haired white man, who spikes the ball over the net, earning our team another point.

My team high fives each other and we rotate to our next positions in the pool. My team won the first game and lost the second, after going point for point with each other. The game is tied up, both teams only two points away from victory.

With the rotation, Blake is up to serve and I'm in the front, at the net. Across the net, Cyrus grins at me, "Don't take this loss too personally, beautiful."

Beautiful? That's new, but I don't take the time to think about it, shrugging it off as something he probably said to try to knock me off my game.

I scoff, "The game ain't over yet."

The referee signals for Blake to serve, and he serves an ace. My team celebrates the point before the ball is returned to our side and Blake serves again. Cyrus's team easily returns the serve, sending the ball back over the net to us. The ball is bumped and set and headed to me to get over the net. Expecting me to try to spike the ball, Cyrus jumps up to block, but instead I use my fingertips to tip the ball over the net, just past his reach, and it lands in the water without being touched.

"And that's game!" The referee calls out.

My team erupts into cheers and high fives over our victory.

"Great job Cass," Maia says with a high five.

"Thank you."

"C'mon, get a drink with us winners."

Out of the pool, I stop by my lounge chair to grab my towel and dry off before heading to meet Maia at the bar.

"Cass, these are my sisters Amber and Alana," Maia says introducing me to two women standing by the bar. Amber and Alana are clearly twins with identical faces and light brown skin.

I wave at them both, "Hey it's nice to meet you."

Maia orders a round of tequila shots for everyone.

"To the winners, and better luck next time boys!"

"What happened to only drinking dark liquor?" I ask,

looking at Cyrus.

Cyrus holds eye contact with me, "Sometimes you have to know when to make an exception."

My body buzzes at his words, as he smirks at me before he takes his shot. The warmth in my lower belly causes me to clench my thighs together.

Get it together Cassandra.

Instead of replying to him, I toss my own shot back, grimacing at the burn.

"Well it was really nice to meet you guys."

"What, no!" Maia exclaimed. "You don't have to leave."

"Baby, she didn't sign up to be stuck with us all day," Blake says with a chuckle wrapping his arms around Maia's waist.

"I didn't want to intrude on you guys' celebration. I was just going to go lay out by the pool."

"We were going to do that too, right," Maia says, aiming the question at her sisters.

"Girl yes, I could use some sun," Amber replied easily.

"Then it's settled we'll go with you."

I laugh at Maia, but accept her and her sisters' company, honestly grateful to not have to be alone. We head back to where I had been sitting earlier, and luckily there are a few other open seats that we are able to push to all be next to each other.

After a little while, Maia breaks the comfortable silence that had fallen between us.

"Soooo, how do you and Cyrus know each other again?" Maia asks after a few minutes of quiet.

She honestly lasted longer than I expected before asking about me and Cyrus.

Me and Cyrus? Since when has there ever been a, 'me and Cyrus'?

"We've known each other since we were kids, and went to school with each other up through high school. But we haven't seen each other since graduation."

"Interesting."

"What do you mean, interesting?" I ask, curious about whatever she was trying to imply.

"Nothing. He just seems real interested in catching up with you."

"Nah it's not even like that."

"Mmhmm," she says noncommittally. "If you say so."

For the rest of the afternoon, we all lay out and relax. We share some snacks and drinks brought by the poolside waiters and get to know each other. Maia is really nice, and so are Amber and Alana, and we hit it off quickly.

"So what are you doing for dinner?" Maia asks when we're standing up to leave the pool.

"Oh, I was planning on checking out one of the resort restaurants."

"We rented out a part of the beach for a group dinner with our friends and family. You should join us."

"No, no," I say quickly. "I don't want to intrude on your trip and I'm really okay."

"Girl its not an intrusion, you're really cool and it'll be a fun time," Amber offers.

Before I can say anything else Maia continues on.

"It starts at 6. Just think about it, okay?" Maia stands, wrapping her towel around her body. "Plus I'm sure that Cyrus would love to see you."

"What are the fucking odds that they're here?" I say to Tiffany over FaceTime explaining the events of the past two days.

"And now I'm invited to this dinner with them, and I just don't think any of this is a good idea."

"Why not?" She asks. "You get to hang out with a fine ass man and some other people that you said yourself seemed really nice. I'm not seeing the problem here."

"The problem," I huff. "Is that this is not how this trip was supposed to go. I was supposed to be here drinking mojitos and relaxing alone. Not running into old classmates and their family."

"Ah yes, you have a good time with a fine ass man and his nice family invites you to what's probably going to be a bougie ass dinner. You're right, life is soooo hard."

"That is not the point!" I try to reason.

"Girl bye, I am not here for your foolishness. Either you want to go and have a good time, and then ride the man's dick after, or you don't, it's very simple."

"Tiffany!"

"What?! I'm not saying marry the man. You're in Mexico, it's okay to just have a little fun."

I roll my eyes at her.

"C'mon Cass, you have never in your life done anything spontaneous ever," Tiffany says with humor in her voice. "If it isn't fully thought out, with a carefully made and color coded pros and cons list, you're not doing it."

"A girl makes one pros and cons powerpoint and she never hears the end of it," I say with a laugh.

But I know she's right. I like lists and plans and being prepared rather than jumping into something unknown. I've been called "uptight" or "controlling" by more than one ignorant ass man, simply because I value plans and productivity.

"Honey, I know you're scared but let's not block your blessings."

"Fineeee," I concede.

"Great, now get off your ass and let's see those outfit options," Tiffany says, clapping her hands. "That man isn't gonna know what hit him when he sees you.

6

CYRUS

"So Cassandra, huh?" Blake asks, leaning back in his chair.

Blake and I decided to sit on the patio by the beach while we waited for the others to get ready before dinner. Will and Damian joined us a little while later, and to no one's surprise, the girls still weren't ready.

"Man, you and your wife just gotta stay all in my business," I reply to Blake with a chuckle.

"Things looked a little heated during the game earlier. I didn't know that y'all had kept in touch."

"We didn't. Before last night, I hadn't seen Cassandra since graduation."

"So what's up? You on that, or you gonna let her slip past again?"

Growing up, I had a crush on Cassandra all throughout high school, but she never returned any interest. We didn't run in the same circles at all, and in the few classes we had together, we each had our own friend groups that we stuck with. During our senior year, I had finally decided to tell her how I felt, but things didn't end up working out that way.

"You gone finally let her know how obsessed your ass was

with her back in the day?" Blake teases.

"Aight now, I wasn't obsessed."

"Nah I ain't tryna hear that," Blake says. "You were all about that girl, even when you were talking to someone else."

I shake my head at Blake's retellings of the past events, even though he isn't wrong. Back then, if Cass had given me the time of day I for sure would've dropped any other girl for her.

"I'm not even sure I'm going to see her again."

"But you want to, right?"

"Hell yeah," I say confidently. "Man, spending time with her last night, it was like no time had passed."

"Wait a minute, nigga you saw her last night too?"

"Yeah bro, after dinner I went and had a few drinks at the bar and there she was," I explained.

"Damnnnnn."

"Yeah, but I don't know if she's even still here. For all I know, she could be gone already."

Blake raises his eyebrows at something over my shoulder before he gives me a knowing look. "I don't know about that."

I turn around to see what he's looking at, and for a moment, I'm frozen in place. Amber and Alana are walking our way, and behind them Maia is in conversation with Cassandra, laughing at something she's said.

What the fuck.

She's wearing an orange two piece set. The short sleeves of the top hang off her shoulders, leaving her shoulders bare and her breasts on full display. The matching skirt goes all the way to her ankles, but the high slit on one side bares her entire leg. When she looks at me, I hold my gaze with hers, stuck in her trance until she reaches me.

"Hey," she says softly.

"Hey yourself," I smile at her.

"Maia asked me to come, well damn near forced me," Cass says with a chuckle. "I hope that's okay."

"Of course it's okay, Mighty Mouse," I stand and take her hand. "C'mon."

The sun is just beginning to descend in the set, basking the beach in a warm glow. The dinner space is tastefully decorated with white tablecloths on standing tables, candles and floral centerpieces. A large buffet table is off to one side, and the DJ and dance floor are in the middle.

"This is beautiful."

Other guests are just beginning to arrive when we make our way over. We stand at one of the high top tables eating appetizers from waiters walking around the space. Occasionally one of my family members comes up to talk, but mainly its just me and Cass talking with each other.

The soft background music that had been playing behind the chatter in the space fades out, and Blake's voice comes over the speakers.

"If I could just have everyone's attention for a few minutes."

Blake and Maia stand in the middle of the dance floor and Blake speaks into a microphone.

"Maia and I just really wanted to thank y'all for making the trip out and being here to celebrate with us. Please have some food and drinks and have a great night." Blake holds up his drink in cheers and the rest of us join in.

The DJ turns the music back up and the night truly begins.

"Hey, Cyrus, come here for a minute!" One of my cousins calls out from a few tables away.

I look to Cassandra to see if she's okay.

"Go, I'll be fine."

"You sure?"

Cassandra shoos me away, saying that she was going to get herself a drink. I know that she'll be fine, but I still hate leaving

Cassandra's side, and my body misses the contact of having her close to me. I make my way over to my cousin and get wrapped up catching up with my family. We take pictures and I say hello to aunts and uncles I don't get to see often, engaging in small talk about the things going on in our lives. Eventually, I find a good time to excuse myself from the conversation, intending to get back to Cass.

"I like her for you," Maia says next to me.

"Huh?"

I follow her gaze across the beach and I see Cassandra engrossed in a conversation with someone at the bar.

"You just met her," I reply.

"Yeah, but I get good vibes from her. I see the way you look at her, and the way she looks at you when she thinks no one is watching. Plus she was on my team when we whooped your ass in volleyball."

"Relaaax," I chuckle. "It was only two points, and your ass couldn't even get a serve over the net."

"Okay, not too much now."

I shake my head in laughter at Maia's response. I can't even deny that my feelings for Cassandra are starting to grow, and I would be lying if I said I didn't want to spend more time with her.

Someone calls Maia's name and she gets whisked off to somewhere else and I make my way over to Cassandra.

By the time I reach her, she's alone standing at one of the high top tables sipping her drink.

"Are you enjoying yourself?" I ask, stepping up beside her and leaning my arms against the table.

"Surprisingly I am."

I take the time to take her in. She's pulled her braids up into a bun, but a few curly strands hang free. Faint tan lines are on her shoulders. Small slivers of skin just a few shades lighter brown, evidence of spending the afternoon in the sun.

"You're staring again."

Cass locks her eyes with mine.

"I can't help it, but I'll stop if you want me to."

Her breath hitches and I watch her look away, bringing her glass to her lips and taking a large sip.

"When do you leave?" I ask, drawing her attention back to me.

"In three days," she replies. "You?"

"Same. The wedding is tomorrow, and then I planned to spend some time with my family before heading back."

Two more days.

It sinks in for me just how little time we have. Cass and I went nearly a decade without seeing each other, and realistically it wouldn't be that crazy for us to never speak again after she leaves.

The current song playing through the speakers fades and the beginning notes of the "Cupid Shuffle" plays. The DJ comes on the mic, encouraging everyone to get onto the dance floor.

"Do you want to dance?"

Cassandra looks over at me, biting her lip, contemplating her response.

"C'mon," I urge, and eventually she puts her hand in my outstretched one and lets me lead her to the dance floor.

We find a space to join in, and fall in line with the steps.

Another line dance plays, and we stay and continue to dance. When I look over at Cassandra, her happiness is apparent all over her face. She's relaxed, a hint of a smile on her lips, and she looks absolutely beautiful.

At the end of that song, DJ announces that he's going to switch things up a little bit, and the beginning notes of a very familiar song begins to play.

Cassandra cuts her eyes over to me, "Did you do this?"

I raise my hands in mock surrender. "It wasn't me."

Even though I didn't have a hand in it, I can't help but be

happy and send thanks to whatever forces are at play, and vow to give the DJ a great tip.

"I ain't never had nobody show me all the things that you done showed me..." Cass sings.

I take over after the chorus, singing the first verse. Cass and I go bar for bar with each other, singing along and joking with each other as we sing.

Cass and I end up spending most of the night on the dance floor together, dancing and singing along to everything. My cheeks hurt from smiling and laughing, and I honestly can't remember the last time I had so much fun with someone.

Tonight, when I offer to walk with Cassandra back to her room, she doesn't argue.

When we reach her door, she turns to face me, a smile on her lips. "I wasn't planning on taking Maia up on her offer, but I'm really happy that I did."

"Why, were you not going to come?"

"Because I didn't want it to be weird. We haven't spoken or seen each other in years, and I didn't want to just pop up and barge into your life, especially at a family event like this."

At those words I realize that she has absolutely no idea.

"The girl I had the biggest crush on, for years, happens to be at the same resort as me at the same time, and she takes time to spend time with me and my family. There's no situation in which I would ever be mad about that Cass," I say sincerely.

"What? What does that even mean?"

"It means exactly what I said. I've liked you since high school and I tried telling you, but you weren't hearing me."

Confusion crosses her face. "What? No, that's not how things were at all."

"So you don't remember our senior trip. We spent almost the whole day together at the amusement park, and before we got on the bus to go home I told you that I liked you."

I can see the wheels in her head turning as she tries to

remember the events that I described.

"How was I supposed to know you were serious? You literally always joked around about everything."

"Because I have always been serious about you Cass, you just never believed me. But I understood. All of senior year you had talked about being focused on your future, on making it out of Oak View and accomplishing your dreams, and I wasn't going to stand in the way of you doing that."

She goes quiet, her facial features softening with the impact of my words. I step forward, crowding into her space, using my hand to gently lift her chin to look into her eyes. "But never think for a second that I'm not interested."

Our breaths mingle. I search her eyes for any indication that she's not interested. That I should back away and leave her, to go another decade without seeing or speaking to one another. But I don't see that.

I lean down and take her lips with mine, softly at first, until she opens for me, and any possibility of me walking away from her disappears.

7

CASSANDRA

Cyrus kisses me with fervor, our lips and tongue clashing. He steps closer, eliminating any remnant of space between us, my back pressed fully to the door of my room. I can feel his dick pressed against my stomach and my nipples pebble, straining against the thin fabric of my top. His hand goes around my waist to caress my ass and I can't help the small moan that escapes my lips.

Fuck.

I kiss him back harder, seeking more of the intoxicating pleasure of his lips. Eventually we pull away from each other, both breathless, panting to get oxygen into our lungs.

Cyrus leans down, placing his forehead against mine. "Open the door."

I fumble with my small clutch, trying to find the keycard to my room. Finally I see it and pull it out, placing it over the card reader until I hear the click of the lock disengaging.

As soon as we're in the room Cyrus is on me again, he lips crashing down on mine. I push up onto my toes, kissing him back, but Cyrus puts his hands under my ass and lifts me up to be eye to eye with him. I wrap my legs around his waist and can't help but grind my pussy against his hard erection.

He lets out a groan, "Fuck, Cass."

Cyrus carries me over to my bed, gently setting me down and kissing down the side of my neck. He returns to my lips, kissing me hungrily and hurriedly, as if he can't get enough.

My body is on fire as Cyrus' hands roam over me. He uses both of his hands to cup my breasts, flicking over my already hardened nipples. Cyrus pulls my top up over my head, freeing my breasts. I let out a whimper when he takes one of my nipples into his mouth, sucking and nipping, before easing the pain with a flick of his tongue.

I move my fingers over the buttons of his shirt. When the last button pops free of the shirt, Cyrus stands and shrugs out of it, dropping it to the floor. He reaches up and pulls off the t-shirt he had under his button down.

Cyrus kneels on the floor and pulls me to the edge of the bed. I sit up on my elbows and watch as his hands dive under my skirt and pull my panties to the side. He uses his middle finger to slide through the wetness of my pussy.

"Shit Cass, all of this for me?"

I can't answer, too overwhelmed by the pleasure flowing through my body as Cyrus runs his finger against my slit, over and over and over again.

I fall back onto the bed and let out a moan at his continued movements, aching for more.

Cyrus presses his thumb against my clit. "Use your words."

"More," I whimper.

Cyrus sinks two fingers into my pussy and I gasp at the sudden intrusion. I watch as he fingers me, his fingers getting more and more slick as he plunges them in and out of me. He drops his mouth to my pussy and devours me.

I fall back against the bed and grip the sheets, the intense feelings rushing over my body as his fingers and tongue continue to overwhelm my senses. I try to pull away from him.

But he doesn't let me, he uses his free hand to hold me in place as he continues the overwhelming assault on my body.

"Come, baby." He instructs, replacing his tongue with his thumb and applying just the right amount of pressure.

And then, I am. My breath catches as my body releases and waves of pleasure over me.

Cyrus rises from his knees to his full height, bringing the impressive bulge in his shorts back into view. In one swift movement he discards his shorts and briefs leaving his dick hanging free.

It's beautiful, long and thick, with pronounced veins running along it. I lick my lips as precum leaks from his tip. When I look up at Cyrus' eyes I half expect him to make a joke about me staring at his dick, but the look on his face has me clenching my thighs tight. His eyes are dark and wild as if he's barely containing himself.

"Like what you see?" I ask just barely above a whisper.

Instead of answering me, he fishes his wallet out of his pants and makes quick work of taking out a condom and covering himself. He climbs onto the bed pushing me down flat onto my back and raining kisses down the side of my neck.

"So fucking beautiful."

He slides in in one fluid motion, causing me to gasp at the sudden fullness. His strokes are slow, pulling almost all the way out before easing back in. I dig my fingers into his shoulders as he picks up the pace, holding my hips as he pushes into me over and over.

The sensations brings tingles to my skin, goosebumps rising on my arms from the pleasure. I let out a moan as I pinch my nipple, rolling the hard nub between my fingers.

"Fuck," I gasp.

"Come on this dick." Cyrus tilts my hips, raising me ever so slightly higher, so with every thrust he's hitting me right in the perfect spot, my climax building. "Give it to me."

My orgasm takes me by surprise. It takes over my entire body and fills it with pleasure, until all I can do is fall back on to the bed as Cyrus reaches his own climax as well.

8

CASSANDRA

I wake up with Cyrus' warm body pressed to my back, his arm slung over my stomach, holding me in place against him. At some point last night before falling asleep, I pulled on his t-shirt to fall asleep in. His scent is all around me, and I would have expected it to be jarring, but it isn't.

Why isn't it jarring?

"Stop worrying," Cyrus says groggily, breathing into my neck. The last remnants of sleep cling to his voice, leaving a husky rasp.

"I'm not worrying."

"We both know your mind started going a thousand miles a minute as soon as you opened those pretty brown eyes of yours."

I silently chew on my lip because even though I want to argue, he's right. I slide out of Cyrus' arms and lay flat on my back staring up at the ceiling.

"Two days ago we hadn't spoken in nine years, and now you just woke up in my bed."

"Mhmm."

"So you're telling me you don't think this is absolutely

crazy?"

My mind is going a million miles a minute trying to process all that has happened in the last few days.

"You want to know the honest truth?"

Cyrus' question knocks me out of the spiral my brain was trapped in, and I try to focus on him, instead of the worry filling the back of my mind.

"No, I don't think it's crazy. Because I'm not thinking about any of that." He leans down over me and places a kiss on my neck.

"I'm thinking that I had an amazing night with a beautiful woman." Cyrus leaves more kisses on my neck, venturing lower to my collar bone.

"And had the pleasure of waking up next to her today, and with those two things I'm happy." Cyrus pulls my nipple into his mouth, sucking hard. My body responds, my back arching off the bed to get impossibly closer, a moan escaping my lips. He releases my nipple and looks into my eyes.

"We don't have to have it all figured out Cass, but we can enjoy the moment while we're in it."

"I don't even know what that means."

"It means we just live. We do what we want because that's all we can do."

I play his words over and over in my head trying to make sense of them. To try to hear them and take them in, even though every fiber of my being wants to fight against the idea of jumping in head first without a plan.

Instead of responding with my own words, I grab the sides of Cyrus' face and bring him closer, closing the distance between us until our lips meet. Kissing Cyrus felt like the first sips of a warm drink after being in the cold for too long. My body instantly melts into him, softening to his touches.

My phone rings but I don't reach for it. Instead I enjoy Cyrus, savoring this moment between us until finally my phone goes silent.

Less than a minute later my phone starts ringing again.

Cyrus breaks the kiss. "You should probably get that."

I pout at the interruption, sticking out my lip. Cyrus shakes his head at me and laughs before he climbs off the bed to go to the bathroom. I watch him until he's out of view, my eyes stuck on how good his ass looks covered in his black boxer briefs.

I reach over to my nightstand and grab my phone, and answer the call. Tiffany's face fills my screen.

"You would think that as your favorite sister you would answer my calls to check in on you." Tiffany starts, before catching herself. "What? Why are you looking at me like that?"

Before I can respond, shock and glee cross her face. "Wait a minute, did you actually sleep with him?!"

I cut my eyes to the bathroom. The door isn't fully closed and I can hear the toilet flush.

"Is he in the room with you still?!" She whisper yells, though it's more yell than whisper.

From the bathroom, I hear a low laugh from Cyrus, and a flush of embarrassment rushes over me, my chest and neck getting hot.

"I'll call you later, byeee."

"Wait no I -," she starts before I end the FaceTime.

I swear I'm gonna kill her.

But right now, I stand out of the bed and make my way to the bathroom. I hear the water from the sink turn off as I nudge the door open with my foot.

Cyrus stands at the sink drying his hands with a towel. When I step into the bathroom, he looks up at me in the mirror. Cyrus turns around and leans back against the sink with a smirk.

"You know I'm gonna need my shirt back right?"

I look down at the shirt in question, the hem of it falling halfway down my thighs, making it more like a dress than a shirt.

I smirk at him before I grab the hem of the shirt, pulling it over my head and leaving my body bare. Cyrus' gaze drops to my body, his eyes slowly looking over me before coming back up to meet mine.

I thrust out the shirt towards him to take. "Here you go."

Cyrus reaches out and takes the shirt, but before I can back away he grasps my wrist and pulls me to him. My body collides with his, and I squeal in shock at the action.

"Your pretty ass is gonna make me late."

I palm his already hard dick through his boxers, slowly moving my hand up and down over the length of him.

I smile up at him innocently. "I can stop if you want."

"Or, I can do this," I say, sinking to my knees.

I ease his boxers down until his dick pops free. I wrap my hand around the base of his dick and look up to meet his gaze. His eyes are filled with heat and laced with so much desire, my pussy throbs at just the sight. I hold eye contact with him as I lick the beads of precum oozing from his tip.

I smile at his sharp intake of breath, and take him into my mouth. I hum in appreciation as I wrap my lips around his dick, swirling my tongue around the tip. I slide my mouth down the length of him, bobbing my head as I suck his dick.

Cyrus puts a hand against the back of my head, stilling me before he starts to thrust into my mouth. The tip of his dick hits the back of my throat, gagging me, but I don't pull away.

"Shit." Cyrus hisses, stepping back and pulling me to my feet. He turns us both towards the mirror, his front to my back.

I wiggle my ass against him, teasing, with a wicked grin on my face. Suddenly, he pushes me forward, bending at the waist until my breasts are pressed into the cool surface of the counter.

Cyrus runs the swollen tip of his dick along my wet slit. "If this is what you wanted, all you had to do was ask."

I squirm, trying to push back against him, but the firm grip he has on my waist holds me in place.

"I don't have another condom, beautiful. But I'm clean and I haven't been with anyone since I last tested, except you."

I look at him in the mirror, still pushing my ass into him. "Me too."

As if my words were the key to the last pieces of his restraint, Cyrus kisses down my neck and over the top of my shoulder, while bending me over. In one fluid motion, Cyrus slams into me, stretching and filling me. He kisses the top of my shoulder, giving me only a moment to adjust. I lean up on my hands and push back into him. He pulls out, leaving just the tip until he pushes into me again.

"So damn impatient."

He strokes me deep, the thick length of him hitting just the right spot. His grip on my hips tightens as he pulls me back into him with each thrust.

My speech becomes incoherent. Every yes, more, and oh god, all jumbling together as I get closer and closer to release. Cyrus places a finger against my clit, moving in circles, and using just the right amount of pressure that I'm sent overboard.

My body tenses as I come, pleasure washing over me leaving me whimpering.

"Fuck, baby."

Cyrus gives one final thrust before he pulls out, the warm spurts of his release hitting my ass and lower back.

I lay limp against the counter while Cyrus runs a washcloth under warm water. He gently cleans me up, wiping away the traces of both of our releases. When he's done, he pulls me to him, tilting my chin up to kiss me.

"I want to see you later."

"I guesssss." I tease, drawing out the words.

He lets me go so he can collect his boxers and shirt from the floor of the bathroom, and the rest of his things from the room.

While he dresses, I throw on one of my own sleep shirts and

sit cross legged in my bed.

The click of the door closing behind Cyrus feels like both an ending and a beginning. The end to one hell of a night and morning, but also the beginning of something I still couldn't wrap my head around.

9

CYRUS

After I leave Cassandra's room, I hustle to my own to shower and get my shit together for the wedding. The actual ceremony isn't for a few more hours, but all of the guys were supposed to meet in a designated suite to get ready and take photos. We all agreed on a time that was -

Shit. 30 minutes ago.

I gather the things I need to get ready, including the garment bag with my suit in it, my dress shoes, and leave my room to head to the suite.

"About time your ass showed up." Will opens the door to let me in, and I step into the suite.

"Wow, look who it is," Blake jokes, pulling me into a hug.

The room sets in motion with everyone starting to get ready. Not long after that, the photographer and videographer arrive to start taking the getting ready shots of the groom and groomsmen. We follow the directions of the professionals and take all the pictures before it's finally time for us to go to the ceremony site.

"Alright guys, we need you in your places." The wedding coordinator calls out, poking her head into the room.

I look over at Blake and reach up to fix his tie. "Let's get you married bro."

I've only been to a handful of weddings, but I can honestly say that seeing my brother marry the woman of his dreams is an experience like no other. I'm not the guy who has thought about marriage and kids my whole life. But seeing Blake and Maia, two people I know love each other unconditionally, stand in front of all of us and profess their love. It's given me a new perspective. And now, I know its something I do want in my future.

The reception is very similar to the welcome dinner from the other night, except more formal. Guests sit at designated tables for dinner and waiters serve us our dinner. After dinner and the customary dances are done, the dance floor opens up, and we turn up with Maia and Blake in celebration.

I step off the dance floor to grab a glass of water when my mom steps up next to me.

"Hey ma," I say as I lean down to give her a kiss on the cheek. "Have I told you you look beautiful today?"

"You have, but you can say it again," she jokes running a hand over the gold dress she wore as mother of the groom.

I chuckle and shake my head at my mom's comment. "You look great ma."

"I haven't seen much of you here," she says glancing over at me. "Wouldn't have anything to do with that young lady that you were with at the welcome dinner, who you didn't introduce to me, would it?"

Truthfully, I should have seen this comment coming when I didn't make a point to introduce her to my family. Because, if it's one thing my mama doesn't play about, its respect. But at the time, I didn't want to make her being there a big deal or give anyone, including my mother, the wrong idea about what's going on between me and Cass.

Especially when I don't even know what's happening my

damn self.

I take a sip of my water before answering. "I'm sorry ma, that was on me. Cass is an old friend that happened to be here and Maia invited her to come."

"Mhmm," she replies noncomittally.

"I promise."

"If you say so," she says giving me a pat on my shoulder. "I'm gonna go find your father."

I watch my mom leave before I decide to head out of the reception myself. I catch up with Blake and Maia on the dance floor to say goodbye, giving them both hugs and another congratulations.

I knock on her door, a few quick short raps of my knuckles. I don't even know if she's in her room. When I was leaving the reception, I realized that we had never actually exchanged numbers, and I didn't have a way to contact her.

I lift my hand to knock again.

"I don't think she's there." I hear from behind me.

I turn around and see Cassandra standing a few feet behind me. Any words that I had before I turned around escape me once I see her. She's dressed simply in a long pale pink dress with sandals, but she's so fucking beautiful. I reach out to her, pulling her closer by her hand and leaning down to give her a kiss.

"Yeah, I guess not."

"You look nice." Cassandra looks down at my outfit, a tan linen suit and white button up shirt. I had pulled the tie off a long time ago and stuffed it into my pocket.

"Thank you, you look better. I came from the reception because I wanted to see you."

Cass smiles at my words, and I'm sure if it was possible for her brown skin, I would see her blush.

"There's a dance performance that's happening in 30

minutes that I was planning on going to," Cass starts. "If you want to come with me."

"I guess," I joke, mimicking her statement from earlier in the day. "But I need to change out of these clothes first. I'll meet you at the show."

Cass rolls her eyes at me, but I pull her into me for a kiss. The kiss is sweet and slow, as if she's trying to commit every second to memory. And damn if I'm not doing the same.

Everything about Cassandra feels right. The way our bodies fit together perfectly. The way being around her feels like a breath of fresh air. All of it just feels … right.

I leave Cass to go back to my room and change out of my suit into something more comfortable. The dance performance is being held in an outdoor theater. Rows of chairs sit in front of the stage, and towards the back, scrolling on her phone, I see Cass.

The emcee takes the stage and begins to introduce himself and the show. I move through the rows to get to the open seat next to Cassandra.

"Hey," I whisper, dropping a kiss to her cheek before we both turn our attention back to the stage.

The performance is amazing, the dancers are excellent at what they do, and each number is better than the last. But an added benefit that I didn't anticipate, is seeing Cass experience it all. Her eyes stay glued to the stage, and the look of wonder and awe on her face as the dancers execute their routines is a beautiful thing to experience.

We stand with the rest of the crowd to clap for the dancers at the end of the show.

Cass looks up at me, joy written all over her face. "That was amazing."

I reach down to bring her closer to me. "You're amazing, Cass."

10

CASSANDRA

I really did not mean to wake up with Cyrus in my bed again. I fully planned on us going our separate ways after the dance show, but when Cyrus suggested grabbing a drink from the bar as I nightcap, I agreed.

And then after a few mojitos I decided that I did in fact want to ride Cyrus' dick. So I did. Twice. And I don't regret a damn thing.

"Are you hungry?"

I turn towards Cyrus' voice and see him standing at the other end of the bed in nothing but his boxer briefs. My eyes roam over his body, taking in his broad shoulders and flat stomach and the small trail of hairs that leads lower and lower. I squeeze my thighs together when thoughts of last night start to replay in my head. His fingers and tongue and that dick...

"Cassandra?"

I pull my eyes back up to his face just in time to see a smirk appear on his lips.

"Yes?" I answer innocently.

"I asked if you were hungry."

My mouth waters at the thought of food.

"You're so awake for someone who went to bed at the same time I did." I say through a yawn.

Cyrus shrugs as he pulls on his shirt from the night before. "I regularly have to be up at like 4 in the morning for work. I guess my body is used to it."

I scrunch my nose up at the thought of willingly being up that early.

"How about we meet on the patio for breakfast in like an hour?"

I watch as Cyrus finishes getting dressed, and nod my agreement when he looks at me. "Okay."

Cyrus grabs the rest of his things before he leaves to go to his own room to get ready for the day.

I decide to lay in the bed, cuddled under the warmth of the covers for a while longer because, unlike Cyrus, I am not wide awake.

Cyrus.

I play the events of the past few days in my head over and over again, trying to figure out what is even happening and how this is my life.

Because, here I am at a resort in Mexico, enjoying spending time with a fine ass man, like the main character of a movie.

And that just is not my life. But, right now it is, and I would be lying if I said that I wasn't enjoying it.

My stomach loudly rumbles, so I take that as my cue to get up out of my bed and go get ready for breakfast.

It takes me a little longer than an hour to get ready, but I finally make it out of my room to meet Cyrus. Choosing what to wear took way longer than it should have, because even though I am a chronic over packer, nothing felt right. Ultimately, I decided on a sky blue bikini with a white cover up.

Cyrus is standing off to the side, looking down at his phone, when I reach the patio where breakfast is held.

"Hey," I say grabbing his attention.

The smile he gives me melts my insides a little. Its so genuine and sweet.

"Ready?"

I nod and he takes my hand as we walk to the hostess stand to get a table. We split off from each other to go through the different buffet lines to get our food. When we sit down, the waitress asks if we would like mimosas and I gratefully accept one.

"So what do you have planned for your last day here?" Cyrus asks after he's taken a bite of his french toast.

"Well, Tiffany and I were supposed to do some excursions while we were here, but I didn't really want to do them alone. So I just planned to stay by the pool everyday and relax."

Cyrus nods in understanding.

"You know, except for those days where I get roped into pool volleyball," I joke.

"Hey that ain't have shit to do with me," Cyrus says lifting his hands in mock surrender. "I was just trying to have a nice conversation. You were the one who volunteered."

"You're right. And we won." I reply, gloating just a little bit.

"Y'all got lucky that's all."

"What are you trying to say?" I ask, sitting back in my chair and taking a sip of my mimosa.

"All I'm saying is," Cyrus says, following my lead and sitting back in his own chair with his glass. "You can't do it again."

I know Cyrus is goading me but I let him. Not necessarily because I'm that confident on my own pool volleyball skills, but because if there's one thing about me, I'm not going to back down from a challenge.

I hold the hand that isn't holding my mimosa out to Cyrus. "I bet I can beat you again."

"And I bet you won't." He says, taking my hand in his and shaking it.

We finish our breakfast and hangout by the pool until it's time for the daily pool volleyball game. Cyrus' friends Will and Damian join us again. Will joins Cyrus on his team again, but Damian decides to be on mine. The resort worker in charge of running the game blows the whistle and the game starts.

Not only does my team win, we wash them. We win in two straight games that aren't even close.

"Shit we didn't even have a chance," Will says when we all exit the pool together.

"Better luck next time boys."

"Yeah, yeah." Cyrus responds laughing.

Around the pool is packed when we finish the volleyball game with pretty much every seat taken by someone. Will and Damian decide to leave us to go to the bar.

"You want to go down to the beach? There's probably less people there than here." Cyrus offers.

"Sure."

We walk down to the beach and Cyrus was right, there are significantly less people than by the pool. We easily find two seats to lay our towels out on and sit down. As we lay out, Cyrus and I fall into a comfortable silence. The kind of silence where neither person feels the need to force small talk for no reason.

I'm laying back in my lounger with my sunglasses on, when two guys in neon yellow t-shirts come up to us.

"Hey guys," One of them says greeting us. "Are you interested in doing any excursions? We've got some pretty cool stuff like jet skis and paddle boarding if you're interested."

I look over at Cyrus, but he gives me a look that says he's leaving the decision up to me.

"No we're okay but thank you." I reply.

"You're sure?" The other guys asks. "We can give you a great deal."

"Yeah, I'm sure," I say with a smile.

The two men say goodbye to us before they continue on to go talk to other people out at the beach.

"What activities were you and Tiffany going to do?" Cyrus asks looking over at me.

"We had jet skis and ATVs booked."

"So why did you just turn down those guys?"

"The plan with Tiffany didn't work out," I reply. "So I already decided to stay at the resort for this trip."

"Just because the plan didn't work doesn't mean we have to drop everything." Cyrus stands from his chair. "Let's make new plans."

Before I can respond, Cyrus leaves me and jogs to catch up with the two men. I watch him talk to them, but they're too far away for me to be able to hear anything that's being said. Cyrus talks with the guys for a while before he shakes their hands and walks back over to our seats.

"We have a jet ski tour scheduled for two hours from now."

"You can't be serious." I say in disbelief.

"Why?" He asks. "You planned to go jet skiing while you were here and now you still can."

"Yeah but-," I start.

Cyrus sits down on the end of my lounge chair. The humor that's usually dancing in his eyes is gone, instead replaced with a serious expression. "If you want me to I'll go back over there and tell him never mind, I will. But I think you want to go, and I just want you to have a good time."

I want to argue against what Cyrus is saying. But I really did want to ride a jet ski on this trip. I had my mind made up that I was going to do it with my sister, and when that couldn't happen, I didn't even think another plan was feasible.

I lean forward to give Cyrus a kiss on the cheek. "Thank you."

When our reservation comes I'm so excited that I'm bouncing like a kid hopped up on sugar. There are probably about a dozen people including us at the dock where the jet skis are lined up. The tour guides hand us forms to sign. They have the standard, "if shit hits the fan that's on you," and, "you break it, you buy it," disclaimers. Once everyone's signed their forms, we put on our life jackets and get on the jet skis.

Cyrus and I get on jet skis next to each other, and when he looks over at me, he gives a reassuring smile. The tour guides go over the safety instructions with us, explaining all the dos and don'ts, and then we're off.

I knew that I would enjoy jet skiing, but the actual experience is more than I could have imagined. I have so much fun riding over the water. The tour guides lead all of us through a predetermined route, but even with the journey already being decided, the entire ride feels incredibly freeing.

After we bring our jet skis back to the dock, Cyrus helps me off of my jet ski and we walk to return our life jackets to the tour guides together.

"Did you have fun?"

"Hell yeah" I say, beaming, throwing my arms around Cyrus in a hug. "That was so much fun!"

Cyrus hugs me back, lifting me off the ground in the process, "Good, I'm glad you enjoyed it."

11

CYRUS

I set Cass down from our hug and look down into her eyes, searching for any signs of fatigue. "Are you up for a walk?"

She nods and lets me lead her away from the dock. I take her hand in mine as we walk. Neither of us has a specific destination in mind, instead just relishing in the last few moments of time we have here together. We walk mainly in comfortable quiet, neither of us feeling the need to fill the silence. When we reach where the pavement meets the sand, we stop to take our shoes off before continuing on to the beach. The sun has set, but there's still enough light coming from the resort that the beach isn't in total darkness.

We walk a bit away from the entrance to the beach, putting some distance between us and the few other people also on the beach.

Cass stops and looks up at the sky. I follow her gaze and look at all the stars shining back at us.

"My flight is in the early afternoon tomorrow," Cassandra whispers.

The happiness that was all over her face not that long ago is gone. Instead, she stares out into the ocean, watching the waves crash onto the shore, with sadness etched into her features.

There it is... the acknowledgment of the end of her time here. The end of the carefree few days that we got to share here.

I want to ignore her words. To ignore the reality that things change tomorrow. But I know that I can't, that we can't, because whether we want to acknowledge it or not, tomorrow will come.

Cassandra looks at me, and the expression on her face is one I can't place.

"I didn't come here for this. Hell I wasn't even supposed to be here alone." Cassandra pulls her hand from mine and wraps her arms around herself. "Now here I am with feelings I don't know what to do with."

"And what is it that you're feeling?"

"It's been three days Cy. Three!," Cass huffs, exasperated. "And now I'm sad to be leaving because I like you."

Her words hit me hard in the chest.

She likes me.

Her words hit so hard that I don't have any words of my own. Because, she's right, it's only been three days here. But I'd liked Cassandra for so much longer than that. So I opt for the truth.

"I like you too Cassandra," I say. "And I don't want whatever is happening between us to stop when we leave."

I grab her hand and tug her towards me. I cup her face in my hands, tilting her head up to look directly in her eyes.

"I don't know about you, but I have never felt anything like what I've felt these past few days being here with you. Ever. And if this is what it's like to have you for three days, I'd be an idiot not to fight for more."

"We don't even live in the same city."

I see it now. The look in her eyes that I couldn't place before, its fear. "Baby, I don't have all the answers. I'm just asking you to take a chance."

"You're right we don't live in the same city," I concede taking her hands in mine. "But its less than a two hour flight between Indy and Rosewood, and I want to try. I'm willing to try to figure this out because I want you, Cassandra."

"I'm scared," she says, her voice shaky with emotion.

"Why are you scared?"

"Because none of this was supposed to happen!" she says. "Because we're about to go back to the real world when we leave here. Not the fairytale we've been living in here."

Cassandra stops and takes in a deep breath, "Because I don't want to get hurt."

My chest aches when she admits that, because the last thing I ever want to do is hurt her.

"I'm not saying that you shouldn't be scared. But what if everything goes right? What if things don't end badly?"

"We can make a plan," I offer. "Whether its you coming to me or me coming to you. We won't know what will happen if we don't try."

Cassandra studies my face. Her brown eyes looking, searching, for what exactly, I'm not sure.

"Take a chance on us," I whisper.

Cass lets go of my hands and wraps her arms around me, burying her face into my chest. "Okay."

12

EPILOGUE - CASSANDRA

VALENTINE'S DAY

I check my phone again, but just like two minutes ago when I checked it, I have no messages.

"Hey, I'm gonna head out. Are you sure that you don't want to go out with me and Zara tonight?" Laila, the social media manager for Lovely Day, popped her head into my office.

Laila joined the company a few years ago and we quickly became close friends. In previous years, the three of us, me, Laila, and her best friend Zara would all spend Valentine's day together. But this year, I wasn't feeling it. This year I was in a relationship, and I wanted more than anything to be able to spend the day with my man. But that wasn't possible because he had to spend his day working a 4 day trip.

I let out a sigh and close my laptop. We were the last people left in our office space, everyone else having left early, since it was both Friday and Valentine's day.

"Nah, I think I'm just going to go home and watch movies on my couch," I say with a sigh.

"Damn!" Laila storms away from my office. I'm confused by her sudden outburst, but she returns a second later holding a white box that she thrusts in my direction.

"He said you would say that."

"He?"

"Yeah, remind me never to bet on you again, now I owe him $20."

I look down at the box and the perfectly tied red ribbon, and a small smile creeps over my face. I open the box to see half a dozen chocolate covered strawberries with a small note laying on top of them.

Always thinking of you.
-CL

I can't help the grin that takes over my face, and pick up my phone to send a text to Cyrus.

Cassandra
Oh so you're betting on me now

Cyrus
I take it that I won.

Cassandra
Maybe

Cyrus
I learned my lesson about betting against you. Now, My money is always on you.

Cassandra
Thank you for the strawberries

Cyrus
Of course. I gotta go, talk to you later tonight

* * *

I gather my things to leave and lock up Lovely Day behind Laila and I. I make the short drive home to my apartment building on the other side of Rosewood, and ride the elevator up to my floor. I exit the elevator, and sitting right there in front of my front door, is a vase of beautiful pink roses and a bottle of my favorite wine.

This man.

My heart burst in my chest at not only the gifts, but Cyrus' thoughtfulness behind them. We hadn't said that special word yet. For me, it hadn't felt like the right time when we were together, and I didn't want to say it for the first time through FaceTime. But as more time passed, I couldn't deny that the feeling was there.

I bring the gifts into my apartment, setting them on the kitchen island to read the card.

I hope these make your day just a little brighter.
    -CL

I send Cyrus another text, thanking him for the gifts, but it goes unanswered.

Well I guess it's just me and my wine tonight.

I go through my normal after work routine and change into comfy clothes, before I settle into my couch to find something to watch. I'm two glasses of wine into a bad Valentine's Day rom-com, when my phone buzzes with a text.

Cyrus
    Check your door. Your last gift just arrived.

Confused, I get off the couch and slip my feet into my fuzzy slippers to make my way to the door. I swing the door open, and there, standing in front of me, is Cyrus.

"Hey baby."

I stand there in shock for a moment, surprised that he's standing here in front of me and not in some random hotel in Minneapolis like I thought he would be. When I come to my senses, I launch myself at him, jumping into his arms and wrapping my arms and legs around him in a tight hug.

"Oh my god, what are you doing here!?"

Cyrus walks inside my apartment and sets me down.

"Someone switched shifts with me last minute and I was able to fly here instead."

Cyrus leans down and kisses me, so intensely that when we break apart, I'm breathless.

"I have your last gift," he says, opening the duffel bag I hadn't even noticed previously. He pulls out a plush teddy bear with red hearts stitched on its hands and feet and hands it to me.

"I got this one because they called it the 'I love you bear'," my eyes snap up to Cyrus' as he continues. "And I figured that was perfect because, I love you."

My eyes start to water at his declaration. "Well that's good, because I love you too."

* * *

ACKNOWLEDGMENTS

Wow. If you're here it means that you've read my first ever book and I can't say thank you enough. Reading and writing has always been a passion of mine and to now be a published author is a dream I wasn't sure would ever come true. But here we are.

This book challenged me in so many ways and while my name is the one on the cover, this book wouldn't exist without some pretty amazing people who were in my corner every step of the way.

To Alex - I will never be able to put into words my gratitude for everything you do for me every single day. You believe in me when I don't and always push me to be the best version of myself. I would never have been able to do any of this without you and even though I write love stories, ours is my favorite. I love you so much. It is you and me for forever and always.

To Jordan aka JaydoeFTH - I say that you are my best friend but you have truly become like a brother to me. Thank you for all the support that you have given me from the very first moment I expressed any desire to become an author. You putting yourself out there to release your music gave me the courage to do this and I am so grateful. #GMG4L

To Janil & Natasha - Thank you for saving my first drafts of this novella from the delete button lol. Both of you are so incredibly talented and I feel lucky to not only be able to read your works but to also call you my friends.

To Linesse - You have been with me through every single stage of my life and I love you so much. You have always been there, always rooted for me, always shown me nothing but love. You are the epitome of a best friend and I am so happy to be able to call you mine.

To my internet friends and supporters- To this day it still

shocks me that all of you were excited for this book. Before it was even anything other than an idea in my head, you all gave me so much support and I am so thankful. Sometimes I forget that those silly little videos I make are watched by actual people but your kind words of encouragement mean the world to me.

To my dad - I will always remember sitting on the kitchen floor with you binding your books. Thank you for always being there for me even when I didn't know it. I don't say it often but I hope you know I love you.

To my mom - Everything I have ever done has been in hopes to make you proud and I hope that I am doing that. I love you. Rest easy mama.

Printed in Great Britain
by Amazon

24078722R00040